This edition published by Parragon Books Ltd in 2014

Parragon Books Ltd
Chartist House
15–17 Trim Street
Bath BA1 1HA, UK
www.parragon.com

Written by Margaret Wise Brown
Illustrated by Henry Fisher

Edited by Michael Diggle
Designed by Ailsa Cullen
Production by Charlotte McKillop

ISBN 978-1-4723-1790-2

Printed in China

The Fish with the Deep Sea Smile

Parragon

Bath • New York • Cologne • Melbourne • Delhi
Hong Kong • Shenzhen • Singapore • Amsterdam

One fish came up
from the deep of the sea,

From down in the sea a mile.
It had blue-green eyes
and whiskers three,

But never a deep sea smile.

One fish came up
from the deep of the sea,
From down in the sea a mile,

With electric lights
up and down its tail,
But never a deep sea smile.

Down in the sea a mile.